African Fol

Hare, Baboon, and other animals

Susan Viriri

Copyright © 2020 Susan Viriri

All rights reserved.

ISBN: 9798566687353

DEDICATION

This book is dedicated to my parents Mr. Tichaona Cathian and the late Mrs. Ethrida Kadzviti, who moulded me to be who I am today through Christian teachings and good moral values from the African folktales.

The Party

Once upon a time, there was a baboon named Bobby and his nephew Harry the hare. They lived happily with their families. One day, Harry decided to have a family party at his house. He invited his uncle Bobby and his family.

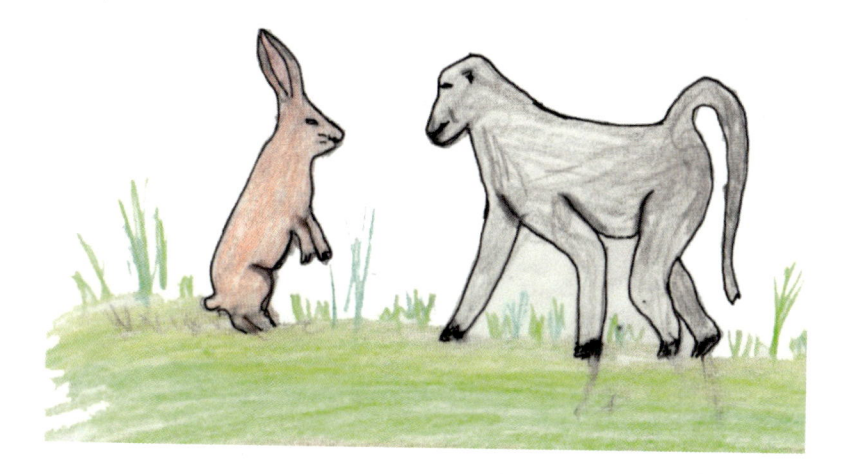

Bobby was so excited to get the invitation. "But there is one condition," Harry said. "What is it?"

asked Bobby. "You have to wash your hands at the river before you come," replied Harry. "That is not a problem," said Bobby smiling.

Bobby went home happily and told his wife and kids. They were all overly excited and looking forward to the party.

The kids could not even sleep that night thinking about the food, the dance and everything that they thought were going to enjoy at the party.

On the day of the party, Harry's wife and kids did all the preparations and cooking of food.

The aroma of the food could be smelt from afar. Harry's wife really wanted to please her guests. Meanwhile, Harry decided to burn all the grass around his house. No-one had the slightest idea of why he was burning the grass. They thought, maybe he is trying to clear the way for the guests, or he wanted to get rid of snakes that could hurt his children, but Harry had a different plan.

Bobby and family made their way to Harry's house. The children were really looking forward to eating, drinking, and dancing. On the way, they were jumping up and down with joy. Bobby's wife thought she could also learn new cooking tips from her friend. They were all looking forward to a great day ahead.

On their way, they had to pass through the river

as they had been instructed.

When they arrived at Harry's place, they found

Harry waiting at the entrance as if to welcome

them. They were so happy to see him and they

thought; *"Oh, what a welcome!"* "I knew you would

come," said Harry with a big smile, "but first, I have to check if you have washed your hands as I told you to." "We have washed as you have asked!", they all screamed. "Let me see!" he insisted.

They all showed their hands but to their surprise they were all covered in ashes from the burnt grass. "As you can see, your hands are all dirty, you need to go back to the river and wash them again," said Harry. Meanwhile, Harry's wife and kids had started enjoying the food. They seemed not to care that their guests were still outside.

Bobby and his family went back to the river grumpily.

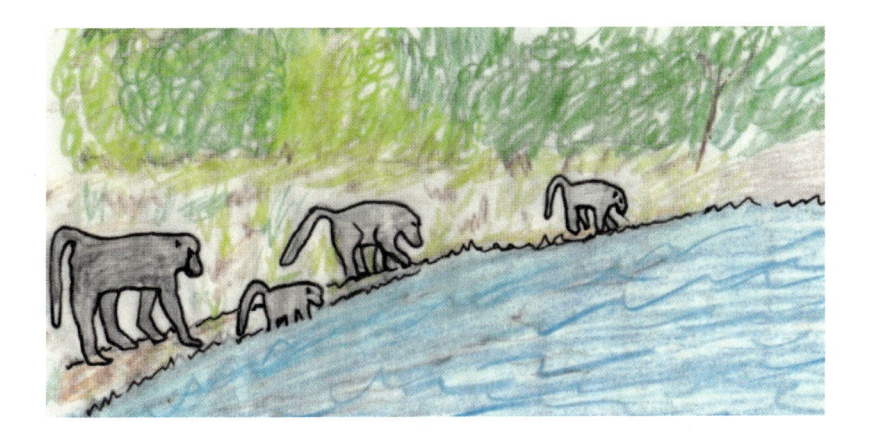

They washed their hands and came back as quickly as they could because the party had already started. When Bobby and family returned, Harry asked to see their hands one more time.

Once again, their hands were all covered in ashes. "I cannot allow you to come in like that!" shouted Harry, "You will have to go back to the river and wash those hands!"

Though they were upset, they all made their way back to the river because they really wanted to attend the party.

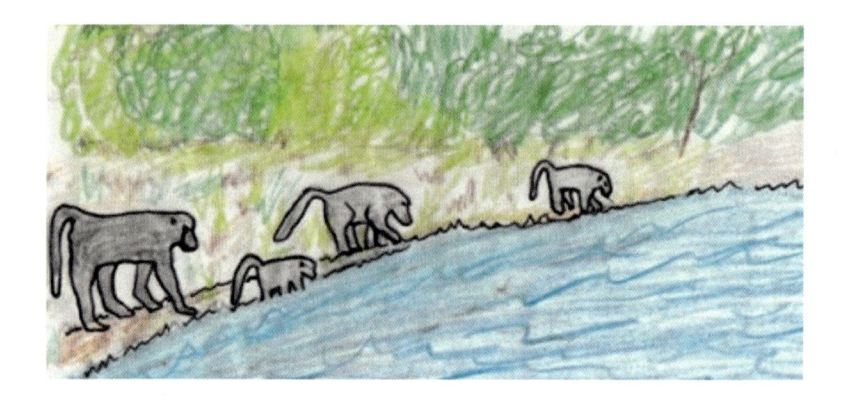

Walking on fours again, their hands got dirty once more. They found Harry still standing at the entrance and asking to check their hands again.

"I don't think you really want to eat my food. You need to go wash your hands again," he said mockingly. "It's not worth it!" Bobby snapped, "The food is almost finished, and you expect us to come back? Never!" Disappointed and hungry, Bobby and his family left and went home. "I will surely get him one day!" muttered Bobby.

That night after dinner, Bobby's family sat quietly thinking of the bad day they had experienced.

Bobby told his wife that he was surely going to revenge. "Time will tell," he said.

It was now the following year and Harry had forgotten the prank he had pulled on his uncle. Bobby however, had not forgotten, so he planned to revenge. He then visited his nephew Harry to invite him to a birthday party for one of his children.

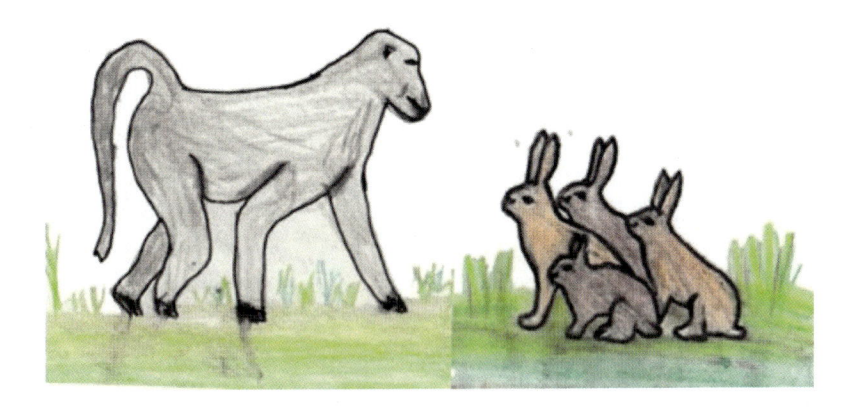

Harry's family was excited about the invitation. The children sang and danced with joy.

Harry's wife slept early so that they would wake up early to prepare for the party.

The next day they woke up early and prepared for the great day. They did not even eat breakfast as they expected to eat at the party. They left for Bobby's place full of joy.

On arrival, they found Uncle Bobby and his family sitting in a tree. Bobby's wife and kids were busy eating and singing merrily. Bobby knew that his nephew Harry and family could not climb trees, yet he decided to hold the party in a tree.

They looked up, not believing what they were seeing. How could Uncle Bobby do this to them. "Unfortunately, this is a tree house party, and you have to climb up if you are here for the party,"

scoffed Uncle Bobby. Harry could not hold his anger. He lashed out at his uncle and told him how he had belittled him in front of his children. Uncle Bobby grinned and only said, "What goes around, comes around!"

Harry was so angry and ashamed of what he had done to Uncle Bobby's family before. He told his wife and kids that they should leave. They all left with their heads hanging down with shame.

Moral of the story: Do to others what you would like them to do to you.

"Sneak, sneakity, sneak"

Once upon a time, there lived Harry the hare and his uncle Bobby the baboon. They lived in a forest near a certain village. One year, there was famine and so much hunger that Harry decided that they should go to a nearby village and steal some milk from people's cows.

"I don't think that's a good idea," argued Uncle Bobby. "What if we are caught? Those people won't spare our lives." "We will not be caught," replied Harry, "I have a good plan uncle." After a long time of discussion, they finally agreed to go ahead with the plan. "But you have to go first," said Uncle Bobby. "No problem," replied Harry, "You will see how skillful I am."

Early next morning, Harry took a large jug and headed for the village. As he approached the village, he started walking slowly, counting three steps while whispering to himself; *"Sneak, sneakity, sneak ……., sneak, sneakity, sneak ……,"* so that he would not alert the dogs of his movements or else the people would wake up.

Luckily for him, no-one heard a sound. He continued until he reached the kraal where the cows were. He quietly went in straight to the cows.

He tied the back legs of one cow and started milking. He did that from one cow to another. He was pausing and listening if there were any noises as he continued milking. He filled his jug and was extremely happy. He sneaked out of the kraal again and started walking the same way going back home.

"Sneak, sneakity, sneak…., sneak, sneakity, sneak," he whispered. He did this until he was out of the village. He started whistling and celebrating all the way home. "What a clever animal I am," he bragged.

Bobby was amazed when he saw Harry with a jug full of milk. "How did you manage?" Bobby enquired. "I told you, it's very easy and you know that I am very clever uncle." Harry put the jug in a safe place and got a cup of milk for each to drink.

They sat down and Harry told Bobby how he did his '*sneak, sneakity, sneak…*' trick. "Wow! Wow!" exclaimed Bobby, "That sounds easy! You never run out of ideas nephew, that's why I love you. I don't think we will ever go hungry again in this season." "I told you," replied Harry with a smile.

A few days later, the milk got finished and it was now Bobby's turn to go to the village. He asked Harry once more about the trick. Harry explained; "When I got to the village, I started walking slowly, saying, *"Sneak, sneakity sneak ...., sneak, sneakity sneak!"* pausing and listening for any movement or a dog bark." "I got it, I got it!" Bobby interrupted. He took the jug and left for the village.

As he approached the village, he started shouting; *"Sneak, sneakity sneak! ..... sneak, sneakity sneak!"* He didn't understand that Harry was whispering to himself when he was sneaking. As he continued shouting, the dogs heard him and they ran towards him, barking. They caught Bobby and started dragging him whilst biting his legs. The noise woke the villagers up and the men ran towards the dogs carrying big sticks. When they got there, they found a baboon lying down with the dogs pulling and biting him. They started beating him with sticks asking him what he wanted from their village

Bobby cried and begged for mercy. "I'm sorry, please forgive me! My nephew fooled me and now I'm in trouble. I will never do it again!" he continued crying. The men later felt sorry for Bobby then chased the dogs away. They told him to leave their village and never to come back again. He thanked them and left for his home. He even forgot to take his jug with him.

Bobby limped back home crying and accusing his nephew Harry of having fooled him. His whole body was swollen and was sore. He was wondering what he had done wrong. He thought his nephew had somehow lied to him.

When Harry saw Bobby coming, he ran to meet him. "What happened?" he asked.

"Didn't you do the *sneak, sneakity, sneak* trick, like I told you?" "That was the problem! you fooled me!" Uncle Bobby snapped. Harry asked his uncle to explain what he did, and Bobby explained. "Oh, my goodness! you didn't get me right!" cried Harry. "You were supposed to whisper and not say it aloud. This was to make sure you stop and listen for any sound coming from the village." Harry laughed but his uncle kept on crying. He was so sad and in a lot of pain that he did not want to talk to Harry till the next morning.

When the other animals heard the story, they laughed at Bobby too.

"What a fool," they said. From that day, they called them; "Clever Harry" and "Foolish Bobby."

Moral of the story: Always follow instructions

Fox, The Wise Judge

Once upon a time, there was a lion named Leo who was causing havoc in a certain village by killing people and other animals. The village Chief then decided that some men should make a cage to trap it. One day, as Leo was roaming around, he saw a big piece of meat lying in a cage and he was tempted to grab it. Little did he know that it was a trap. As Leo entered the cage to get the meat, the cage closed. Leo had no way of getting out. So many days passed without any food or water. Other animals were passing by but were afraid to help him. Leo tried everything he could to get out but failed.

It happened that one day, a man named Jerry from another village was passing by. He had no idea about the trap or about the problems Leo had caused.

When he got closer to the cage, Leo shouted, "Hey Mr. man! Please come and help me…! I have been trapped in here for days now and I am so hungry and thirsty! Please get me out!" Jerry thought for a moment and said, "I don't think I can help you, because if I do, you will eat me since you are so hungry, please ask other animals." "I will do no such thing, please help me and you go your way," begged Leo. Jerry felt sorry for Leo and he opened the cage. **What a terrible mistake that was!**

Leo looked at him and said, "Well, thank you for helping me out, but, because I am so hungry and I don't have the energy to go hunting, I am going to have you as my first meal." "No…, wait! You can't do that. You promised that if I help you will not eat me, now you are going back on your word!" cried Jerry. "Yeah, I did, but it was because I was desperate to get out, but now that I'm out and I am weak, I have no option but to eat you." They argued for a while then Jerry said, "Ok, let us go and find at least three other animals and ask them what they think about this, and if they support you then you can go ahead and eat me." Leo agreed and they started walking, looking for other animals for opinions.

Jerry started praying in his heart that they would meet kind animals to support him. Leo was also praying that they would not meet anyone or that he should at least get support from other animals.

As they were walking, they first met a cow and stopped her.

Jerry cried out, "Hey Mrs. Cow! can you help us solve this problem that we are having?" "Go ahead," replied the cow. "The lion was trapped in a cage and he begged me to free him," Jerry explained. "I helped him and now he wants to eat me. Is that fair Mrs. Cow?" The cow looked down as if she were thinking deeply and she replied, "You people, always use us in your fields, and you take our milk that is meant for our babies. You also kill us for meat to feed your families, so, today, yeah, it's your turn, *be eaten!*" Jerry was puzzled by the cow's answer, but Leo was smiling from inside. They left the wow and continued to walk until they met up with Harry the hare. Jerry was so happy as hare was known to be incredibly clever.

Jerry smiled and said, "Hey Mr. Hare, can you help us solve our problem?" "Yeah, go ahead," replied Harry. Jerry explained how he had helped Leo and now that he wanted to eat him. Harry thought for a moment and said, "Hmm, you people are very cruel too. You hunt us with your dogs and kill us for meat without feeling sorry for us, so yeah, today it's your turn, **be eaten!**" Harry smiled and walked away.

"It seems everyone is on my side," growled the lion, "so why waste time, let me just eat you now."

"No!" cried Jerry, "We are left with one more animal to ask, then maybe, you can eat me."

Finally, they met with the wise Fred the fox. He was walking happily and whistling to himself. "Hello Mr. Fox," Jerry greeted him. "Could you please help us solve our problem?" "Yeah, go ahead," replied Fred, still smiling.

Jerry narrated his story again like he had done to the cow and the hare. "I don't seem to quite understand you," said Fred, "You said you were in the cage and the lion wants to eat you?" "No!" cried Jerry, "It's the lion who was in the cage, not me." "And then?" asked Fred. "I helped him out and now he wants to eat me," Jerry replied. "I don't seem to quite understand you," Fred frowned as if he was confused. Let's go back to the cage then you can show me how it happened."

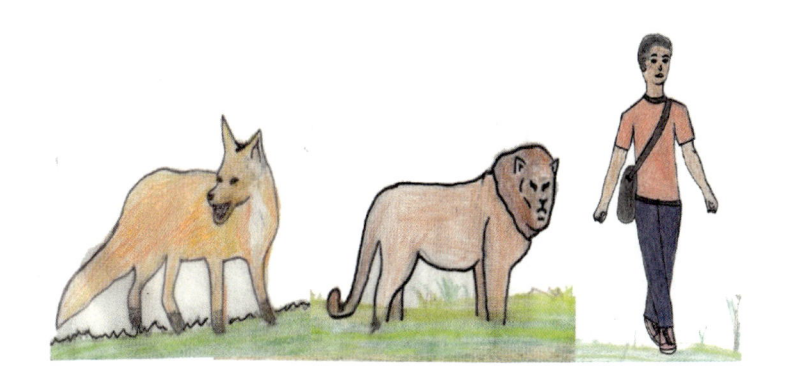

They all walked back to the cage, and when they arrived, Fred said to Jerry, "So, you said you were in the cage?" "No! it is the lion who was in the cage, not me," replied Jerry. "Can you go back Mr. Lion so I can understand the issue here," said Fred. Leo slowly walked back into the cage. "Therefore, was the gate opened or closed when you were passing?" Fred asked Jerry. "It was closed," he replied.

"Now close it so I can see how it was," instructed Fred. Jerry closed and locked the cage as it was before.

"And you, young man, where were you?" "I was just passing by going to my village," Jerry replied. "Great! Case closed!" said Fred with a big smile. "You can now continue with your journey, and you, Mr. Lion, can now rot in there because you are not grateful. Have a nice day!"

Jerry thanked the wise fox and went home. Fred also went his way. Leo was left still trapped in the cage and wondering why he had been so greedy as to want to eat the person who had helped him. No-one knows what happened to him after this incident.

Moral of the story: Always be grateful for all acts of kindness.

The race – Hare and Tortoise

Once upon a time, the wild animals gathered for a get together party and they were eating and drinking happily. Hare started mocking tortoise and challenging to race with him. The tortoise agreed but the other animals thought it was a crazy idea.

The following day, many animals gathered to witness the race. Elephants, zebras, giraffes, lions, hyenas, hippos, skunks, birds, and other animals went to cheer at the finish line.

The fox was chosen to start the race. It was a 2km race which passed through the forest.

Hare and tortoise stood at the starting line and the fox shouted, "On your marks! Get set! …. and he blew his whistle to start the race. Hare took off in a flash speed whilst tortoise took one step at a time.

When hare saw that he had left tortoise way behind, he decided to take a rest under a tree as he knew that it would take a while for tortoise to catch up.

As time went by, he fell asleep. Tortoise slowly walked without stopping. Unknown to hare, tortoise passed him swiftly and kept on walking.

When the animals saw tortoise approaching, they started shouting and cheering and most of them wondering what had happened to hare.

After some time, hare woke up and started running thinking that tortoise was still way back. When he got to the finish line all animals were laughing at him.

Hare was so embarrassed and frustrated to see that tortoise had long arrived and had won the race. He remembered the words he had said to tortoise at the party and could not face him. He left the place without talking to anybody or congratulating tortoise.

He looked for a bush to hide until other animals had forgotten about the event. From that day, he learnt that he should not judge and look down upon others.

Moral of the story: Never look down upon others.

The End